Save Our Squirtle!

#3

PokÉMON junior

D0447357

There are more books about Pokémon for younger readers.

COLLECT THEM ALL!

#1 Surf's Up, Pikachu!

#2 Meowth, the Big Mouth

#3 Save Our Squirtle!

COMING SOON!

#4 Bulbasaur's Bad Day

#5 Two of a Kind

Save Our Squirtle!

POKÉMON junior

#3

By Bill Michaels

SCHOLASTIC INC.

New York Toronto London Auckland Sydney
Mexico City New Delhi Hong Kong

If you purchased this book without a cover, you should be aware that this book is stolen property. It was reported as "unsold and destroyed" to the publisher, and neither the author nor the publisher has received any payment for this "stripped book."

No part of this publication may be reproduced in whole or in part, or stored in a retrieval system, or transmitted in any form or by any means, electronic, mechanical, photocopying, recording, or otherwise, without written permission of the publisher. For information regarding permission, write to Scholastic Inc., Attention: Permissions Department, 555 Broadway, New York, NY 10012.

ISBN 0-439-15420-0

© 1995, 1996, 1998 Nintendo, CREATURES, GAME FREAK.
TM and ® are trademarks of Nintendo. © 2000 Nintendo.

Published by Scholastic Inc. All rights reserved.
SCHOLASTIC and associated logos are trademarks
and/or registered trademarks of Scholastic Inc.

Designed by Joan Moloney

12 11 10 9 8 7 6   3 4 5 6/0

Printed in the U.S.A.
First Scholastic printing, June 2000

CHAPTER ONE

Hit the Water!

"*Pikachu!*" shouted Pikachu. Pikachu was Ash Ketchum's first Pokémon. It was saying, *Hit the water!*

Pikachu was on vacation with Ash. They were on Cinnabar Island. Ash had brought two other Pokémon, Bulbasaur and Squirtle,

with him. He was staying with his friend Brock. Brock's Pokémon Vulpix was there, too.

Pikachu, Bulbasaur, Squirtle, and Vulpix had spent the morning buying souvenirs — maracas, Poké Flutes, and straw hats. Now the whole gang was surfing. All except Squirtle. It was sitting on the beach.

"Bulba bulbasaur," said Bulbasaur, which meant, *What are you waiting for, Squirtle?* Each Pokémon spoke its own language. But they could all

understand one another.

"*Vul vulpix. Vul,*" said Vulpix. *Yeah, Squirtle. Do not be such a baby.*

Squirtle was not going anywhere. It was enjoying itself lying there in the sun. The warm sun made it feel so good. It felt lazy and relaxed. It could hardly keep its eyes open.

"*Squirt squirtle. Squirt,*" said Squirtle. *Leave me alone. I am staying right here.*

CHAPTER TWO

Do Not Move

Pikachu, Vulpix, and Bulbasaur had fun in the waves. But when they came out of the ocean, they did not see Squirtle. It was not anywhere on the beach.

"*Pika pika?*" said Pikachu. *Squirtle, where are you?*

"*Vulpix,*" said Vulpix. *I guess*

Squirtle went home.

"*Bulbasaur-saur-saur*," added Bulbasaur. *I think we hurt Squirtle's feelings. We should not have teased it.*

Bulbasaur and Vulpix felt bad. They had been teasing  with Squirtle about not going in the water. But they should not have made fun of Squirtle.

"*Pika pika pikachu*," said Pikachu. *You should go and tell*

Squirtle you are sorry.

Vulpix leaned down to pick up Squirtle's surfboard. Bulbasaur noticed there was something white on it. Bulbasaur gave a cry. *"Bulbasaur?" What is that?*

There was a note on the surfboard:

If you want to see your friend Squirtle again, you will have to give us the little electric mouse. Do not move till you hear from us.

Oh no! Squirtle had been kidnapped!

No one had signed the note, but they all knew who it was from. Something this bad had to be the work of Team Rocket.

CHAPTER THREE

A Plan!

Pikachu, Vulpix, and Bulbasaur could not believe it. How could anyone kidnap Squirtle? It was one of the sweetest Pokémon. (Except when it was under attack!) How would Squirtle survive?

The Pokémon all knew what

the note meant by "the little electric mouse." That was Pikachu. An electric-element Pokémon, mouse-type. Jessie and James — Team Rocket — were Ash's worst enemies. Along with their talking Pokémon, Meowth, they were always trying to make trouble for Ash. They wanted to steal Pikachu for their boss. Now they had made trouble for Squirtle, too.

Vulpix looked Pikachu in the eye. *"Vul vulpix, vul?"* it said. *Team Rocket wants to trade you*

for Squirtle. Will you do it?

"*Pika pikachu,*" replied
Pikachu. *Of course I will, to save
my friend.*

"*Bulba . . .*" said Bulbasaur.
Unless . . .

"*Vulpix?*" *Unless what?*

"*Bulba! Bulbasaur!*" *Unless
we can save Squirtle ourselves!*

CHAPTER FOUR

A Clue

Just then, Pikachu noticed something. It was a small bubble! And then another! And another! They were all floating in a line on the sand. They seemed to lead somewhere.

"Pika! Pikachu!" said Pikachu. It was very excited. *Look! There!*

"*Vul. Vulpix!*" Vulpix was even more excited. *Squirtle has used its Bubble Attack to leave us a clue!*

"*Bulba. Bulbasaur!*" *Look over there! The little bubbles lead that way!* Bulbasaur pointed to a forest in the distance.

It was true. There was a path of little bubbles. They led away from the beach, all the way to the forest. How smart Squirtle was!

"*Pika!*" *Come on!* Pikachu started toward the forest. Its two friends followed.

"Bulba bulbasaur!" Do not worry, Squirtle! We are coming!

"Vul!" Vulpix let out a roar. *We are your friends!*

Pikachu raised an arm in the air. *"Pika! Pikachu!" And friends always help friends in trouble!*

Bulbasaur, Vulpix, and Pikachu followed the little bubbles to the trees. Inside the forest, the trees

were very thick and crowded.
They shut out the sun. It was a
lot different than a walk on the
beach. In fact, it was a little scary.

CHAPTER FIVE

On Their Own

Vulpix looked back at the beach where Ash was lying in the sun. *"Vul vulpix, Vul!"* it said. *Maybe we should ask Ash to help us.*

"Pika pikachu." Let him rest. He works so hard, and he is tired.

"Bulba. Bulbasaur." Besides,

we can do this on our own.

"Pikachu!" Yes, we are smart enough!

"Vulpix!" And brave enough!

"Bulbasaur!" What are we waiting for? We should go!

The three Pokémon walked farther into the forest. They followed the bubbles Squirtle had left. But walking through the thick forest was not easy. There were vines and branches and big tree roots everywhere.

Suddenly, Bulbasaur had an idea. *"Bulbasaur!" Watch this!*

Bulbasaur used its Razor Leaf Attack. It cut through the branches

and vines. It did it very fast. You could hardly see it happening. But after a minute or so, the path was clear! The Pokémon could now walk through the forest.

"*Vul, vulpix. Vul!*" *Good job! But be careful with that Razor Leaf. It could hurt someone. Like me!*

Pikachu pointed forward.

"Pikachu! Pika!" Come on! We do not have any time to waste!

The three Pokémon marched onward. But Pikachu was right. Who knew how much time they had? Who knew what Team Rocket was going to do to Squirtle?

Just then, things got a lot worse.

There were no more bubbles! They just ended!

Pikachu stopped. It thought it saw something. *"Pika pi!" Look! Up in the tree!*

CHAPTER SIX

A New Friend

The three Pokémon looked up.

Pikachu pointed to a branch.

There was something on it.

It was Spearow!

Vulpix was very excited.

"Vulpix! Vul!" Spearow! Come down!

"Bulbasaur!" We need your

help! Please come down.

Spearow flew down from the branch. Its short wings flapped very hard. It landed on the ground next to Pikachu, Bulbasaur, and Vulpix.

"Spearow!" What brings you three here?

Pikachu explained it all to Spearow. It told Spearow how Squirtle had disappeared. Pikachu talked about the bubbles Squirtle had

left as clues. It told Spearow how they had been following the bubbles, and how the bubbles had stopped. Just like that.

Pikachu looked at Spearow with hope. "*Pika pika chu chu,*" it said. *Now maybe you can help us.*

"*Spear.*" *How can I help? I will do anything for Squirtle.*

"*Pikachu!*" *Go fly high up in the sky. Look for Squirtle!*

Vulpix looked upset. "*Vulpix.*" *That is a good idea. Too bad I did not think of it.*

Spearow started flapping its wings. It flapped them harder. And harder. And harder.

"*Spearow!*" *I will fly up high. I will look everywhere for Squirtle!*

Up and up it went, higher and higher. Soon, Spearow was just a small speck high up in the sky.

The three Pokémon looked at one another. They all sat down and waited. They waited a long time. But they were very hopeful. There must be more clues about where Squirtle was. Could Spearow find

the tiny turtle Pokémon?

An hour later, Spearow came back. It looked sad.

"Spear spearow." I could not see Squirtle. I looked everywhere. I am sorry.

CHAPTER SEVEN

Luck

Spearow flew away. The three Pokémon lowered their heads. They were sad. What could they do now?

"*Vul.*" *I am hungry*. Vulpix's stomach rumbled. The noise was very loud. "*Vulpix?*" *See what I mean*? Vulpix rubbed its tummy.

Pikachu looked at Vulpix and smiled. It walked over to a tree. Pikachu used its Agility Power to climb all the way up to the top. It was looking for apples. It knocked some down for its friends.

On its way down the tree, Pikachu stopped. It had found something!

"Pikachu! Pika!" Look! Here is a mark on the tree! Squirtle must have used its Tail Whip to make this mark.

Bulbasaur jumped up in the air. *"Bulbasaur!"* Now we can follow

the marks on the tree!

Pikachu had six apples. There were two apples for each Pokémon. They tasted so good!

Pikachu, Bulbasaur, and Vulpix were all happy again.

When they were done eating, the Pokémon started off once

more. They followed the marks on the tree. They were easy to see if you looked carefully. On and on the three friends went.

But then the tree markings stopped!

What would they do now? They were very deep in the forest. Ash could not help them. He was far, far away.

Then they heard a noise.

Whip!

It was not very far away.

Whip!

"Pikachu?" What is that?

31

CHAPTER EIGHT

The Cave

"Bulbasaur." I know! That is the sound of Squirtle's Tail Whip.

"Vulpix!" Yes. I know it!

Whip! There was the noise again.

"Pikachu. Pika." We should follow the noise. Then we will find Squirtle!

The three Pokémon followed
the sound. They crawled over
some rocks and under some
bushes. When they came out,
they were standing in front of a
big cave.

Whip!

The noise was coming from the
cave! Squirtle must be inside! But
there was something blocking the
cave. What was it? A huge rock?

No!

It was Snorlax! Sound asleep.

*"Bulbasaur." How can we
move it? It is so big!*

Pikachu tried its Thunder Shock. Nothing happened. Snorlax was just too big! Bulbasaur tried wrapping its Vine Whip around Snorlax. Bulbasaur tugged and tugged.

While Bulbasaur was tugging, something fell to the ground.

It was one of the Poké Flutes the Pokémon had bought at the beach.

"*Pika!*" *Now I remember!* Pikachu picked up the flute.

"*Pika pika pi.*" *This flute music is the only thing that can move Snorlax!*

Vulpix leaned forward.

"*Vul, vul?*" *Fine. But what do we do after Snorlax moves away?*

The three Pokémon looked at one another. It was a good question. Even after Snorlax moved,

they still had to face Team Rocket.

"Pika?" What will we do?

"Bulbasaur." We will make a plan.

"Pika pika." Yes! We will make a plan.

Vulpix rubbed its long tails alongside Bulbasaur and Pikachu. *"Vul, vul." All of us. Together.*

CHAPTER NINE

Rescue!

The three Pokémon huddled together. They talked and talked. Then they talked some more. They worked together. Finally, they had a plan.

Pikachu faced its two friends. *"Pika?" Ready, everyone?*

Bulbasaur and Vulpix nodded.

*"Pika pikachu." Okay, on the
count of three, we will begin.*

One . . .

Two . . .

Three!

Pikachu began playing the flute. The music was beautiful!

But Snorlax did not move.

The three Pokémon looked at one another. Oh, no! Maybe the plan would not work!

Pikachu began playing again.

This time it worked! Slowly, Snorlax woke up. It stretched its arms. Then it moved slowly away

from the cave's entrance.

Inside were Squirtle and Team Rocket!

Boy, did they all look surprised.

Squirtle jumped up and down. *"Squirtle! Squirtle!" You have come! I knew you would!*

Now it was Bulbasaur's turn. In a flash, it used its Vine Whip to

pull Squirtle away from Team Rocket.

"Hey!" said Jessie. "You cannot do that!"

"Not unless we say so," said James.

"*Meowth!* And we do not say so," said Meowth.

"*Vul vulpix.*" *Just watch us!*

Team Rocket started to run after Squirtle. Vulpix took action. It used the powerful flames from its Fire Spin to block them. Team Rocket could not move!

Pikachu and Bulbasaur were very happy. They gave Squirtle a big hug.

"*Squirtle, squirtle!*" *I am free! You set me free!*

Vulpix turned and spoke to the other Pokémon. "*Vulpix! Vul!*" *Run away with Squirtle! I will be right behind you!*

Bulbasaur and Squirtle ran into the woods. They ran back the way they had come. But Pikachu stayed behind. The plan was not over yet!

Pikachu picked up the flute. It began playing again.

The sleeping Snorlax woke up when it heard the music. It began walking back to the cave.

Just then, Vulpix stopped its Fire Spin. Team Rocket started to run out of the cave. But Snorlax sat down in front of the cave! Pikachu stopped playing the flute.

Snorlax went back to sleep. Team Rocket was trapped inside!

Pikachu and Vulpix laughed. They ran and joined Squirtle and Bulbasaur.

The four Pokémon were delighted. They had rescued Squirtle! They had done it as a team. They had worked together! Now Squirtle was safe and sound.

Squirtle smiled at Bulbasaur, Vulpix, and Pikachu. *"Squirt squirtle!"* *Thank you! You*

saved me! I am so happy!

"*Pika pika pikachu!*" *That is what friends are for!*

"*Vulpix.*" *To help one another.*

Just then, the four Pokémon heard a noise.

What could it be?

CHAPTER TEN

A Friendly Face

The noise got closer.

And closer.

"Vulpix?" Who can it be?

"Pika!" Maybe we should
hide!

The four Pokémon did not
know what to do. The noise was
very close. Then someone came

out of the forest. It was Ash!

"There you are!" he said. "I was so worried about you!"

Pikachu ran over to Ash. It put its arms around him.

Ash gave Pikachu a hug.

"What were you guys up to?"

The four Pokémon smiled.

Oh, nothing. Just a day at the beach for us Pokémon.

Some days are just *the pits.*

POKÉMON junior

Chapter Book #4:
Bulbasaur's Bad Day

Some days are just plan bad — others are *the pits.* Just ask Bulbasaur. The Grass Pokémon falls into one of Team Rocket's traps — literally! Meowth has dug a big pit, and now Bulbasaur is stuck inside. When Meowth shows up, it's up to Bulbasaur to defend itself. Can Bulbasaur outwit Team Rocket in time?

Catch it soon in a bookstore near you!

Visit us at www.scholastic.com

©1995, 1996, 1998 Nintendo, CREATURES, GAME FREAK. TM & ® are trademarks of Nintendo. © 2000 Nintendo.

SCHOLASTIC

POKJR999